THE
DARK

BY

LEMONY SNICKET

ILLUSTRATED BY

JON KLASSEN

LITTLE, BROWN AND COMPANY
New York   Boston

Laszlo was
afraid of
the dark.

The dark lived in the same
house as Laszlo,
a big place with a creaky roof,
smooth, cold windows,
and several sets of stairs.

Sometimes
the dark hid
in the closet.

Sometimes
it sat behind
the shower curtain.

But mostly it spent its
time in the basement.
All day long the dark would
wait in a distant corner, far
from the squeaks and rattles
of the washing machine,
pressed up against some old,
damp boxes and a chest of
drawers nobody ever opened.

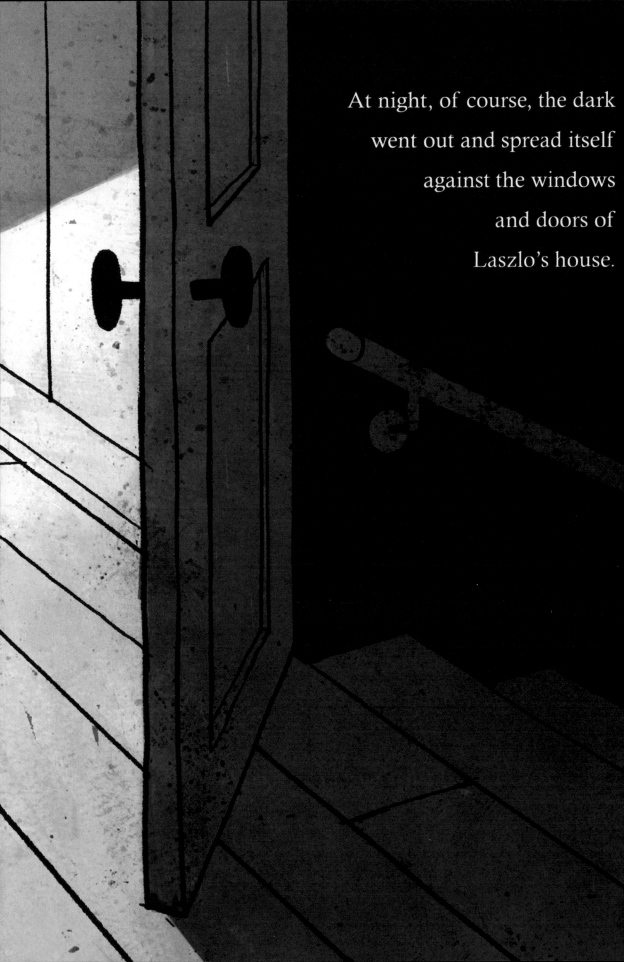

At night, of course, the dark went out and spread itself against the windows and doors of Laszlo's house.

But in the morning
the dark would be
back in the basement,
where it belonged.
Laszlo would peek at the
dark every morning.

"Hi,"

he would say.

"Hi, dark."

Laszlo thought that
if he visited the dark
in the dark's room,
maybe the dark
wouldn't come visit him
in his room.

But one night—

it did.

"Laszlo," the dark said,
in the dark.

The voice of the dark was as creaky
as the roof of the house, and as smooth and
cold as the windows, and even though the dark
was right next to Laszlo, the
voice seemed very far away.

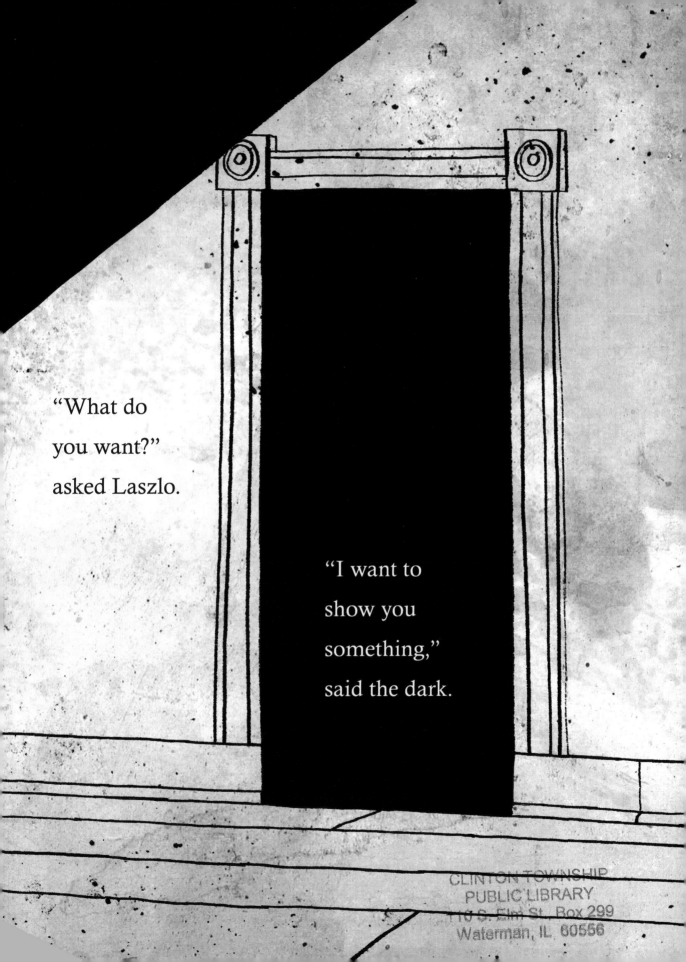

"What do
you want?"
asked Laszlo.

"I want to
show you
something,"
said the dark.

"Yes,"
said the
dark.

In Laszlo's living room was
the biggest window
in the house.
Laszlo looked out at all the
dark outside. Above him
the roof creaked, and he
closed his eyes. Now the
dark was all Laszlo could see.

"No, no," said the dark again.
"Not there."

"Down
here."

"In the
basement?"
asked
Laszlo.

"Yes,"
said the
dark.

Laszlo had never dared come to the
dark's room at night.

"Come closer," said the dark.

Laszlo came closer.

"Even closer,"
said the dark.

You might be afraid of the dark, but the dark is not afraid of you. That's why the dark is always close by.

The dark peeks around the corner and waits behind the door, and you can see the dark up in the sky almost every night, gazing down at you as you gaze up at the stars.

Without a creaky roof, the rain would fall on your bed, and without a smooth, cold window, you could never see outside, and without a set of stairs, you could never go into the basement, where the dark spends its time.

Without a closet, you would have nowhere to put your shoes, and without a shower curtain, you would splash water all over the bathroom, and without the dark, everything would be light, and you would never know if you needed a lightbulb.

"Bottom drawer," said the dark.

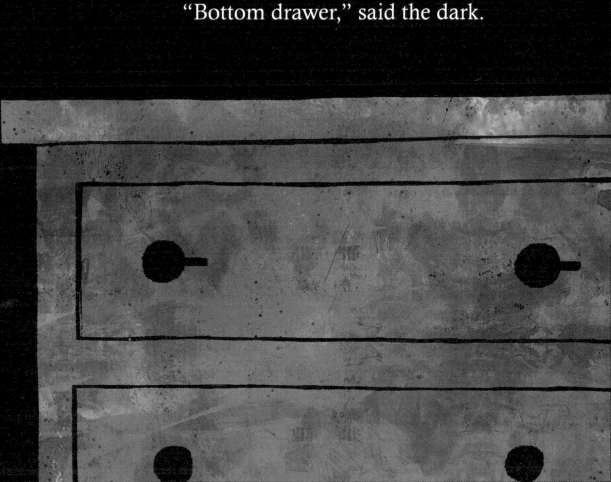

"What?"

"Bottom drawer,"
said the dark.
"Open the bottom
drawer."

"Thank you,"

said Laszlo.

"You're

welcome,"

said the dark.

By the time Laszlo got back into bed,

the dark was no longer in his room,

except when he closed his eyes to go to sleep.

The next morning,
Laszlo visited the
dark in the
basement.

"Hi," he said.
"Hi, dark."

The dark didn't answer,
but the bottom
drawer was still
open, so it looked
like something in the
corner was smiling.

The dark kept on living with Laszlo, but it never bothered him again.

The illustrations for this book were done in gouache and digitally.
The text was set in Calisto MT, and the display type was hand-lettered.

This book was edited by Susan Rich and designed by Patti Ann Harris
and Jon Klassen. The production was supervised by Charlotte Veaney,
and the production editor was Barbara Bakowski.